This Ladybird
Book has been specially
planned to illustrate familiar
objects which a child will
enjoy recognizing and
naming. Helpful suggestions
are included to encourage
comment and conversation
with mother or teacher,
who should talk freely
about the pictures - thus
helping to build up the
child's speech vocabulary.
Baby-talk should always
be avoided.

*The Ladybird Picture Books
are ideally suited for use with
the Ladybird 'Under Five' series—
'Learning with Mother' and its
associated Playbooks.*

A LADYBIRD

Fifth
Picture
Book

by ETHEL and
HARRY WINGFIELD

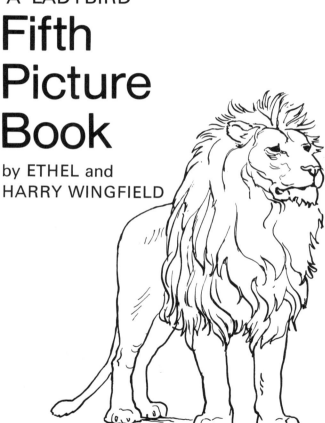

Ladybird Books Loughborough

goat

Talking about goats:

A mother goat is called a "nanny-goat".
A father goat is called a "billy-goat".
A baby goat is called a "kid".

cherries

Talking about cherries:

Cherries grow on trees.
What do we find in the middle of a cherry?
Birds like to eat cherries.

crayons

Talking about crayons:

Shall we count the crayons and say what the colours are?

camera

Talking about cameras:

If you had a camera, what would you like to photograph?

elephant

Talking about elephants:

This young elephant is asking for food.
How will it pick up its food?
Some people ride on elephants.

rose

Talking about roses:

How many rose buds can you see?
Many roses have a sweet smell.
We must be careful of the sharp thorns.

roller
skates

Talking about roller skates:

When you put on these roller skates you have to tie the laces and fasten the buckles.
Can you tie laces and fasten buckles?

meat

Talking about meat:

Somebody is using a knife to carve this meat.
What do we mean by "carve"?
We eat meat after it is cooked, but some animals
eat it raw – that is, not cooked at all. Can you think
of an animal that eats raw meat?

cotton
reels

Talking about cotton reels:

Shall we count the cotton reels in the picture?
Shall we say what the colours are?
What colour cotton is threaded through the needle?

duckling

Talking about ducklings:

A duckling is a baby duck. It has webbed feet. Do you know why?

Have you heard the sound a duck makes?

Can *you* make that sound? Shall we try?

stream

Talking about streams:

This is a stream. Sometimes it is called a brook.
What do you think you might find in it?

hat

Talking about hats:

Shall we point to the fringe around this cowboy hat and say what the colours are?
Can you find a cowboy's gun in this book?

dates

Dates grow on a tree, in big bunches.
They are sticky, aren't they? Perhaps that is why
there is a little fork with this box of dates.
What colour would you say the dates are?
How many are outside the box?

purse

Talking about purses:

This purse fastens with a clasp. Can you point to it?
Can you see the pattern on the purse?
What do we usually put in a purse?

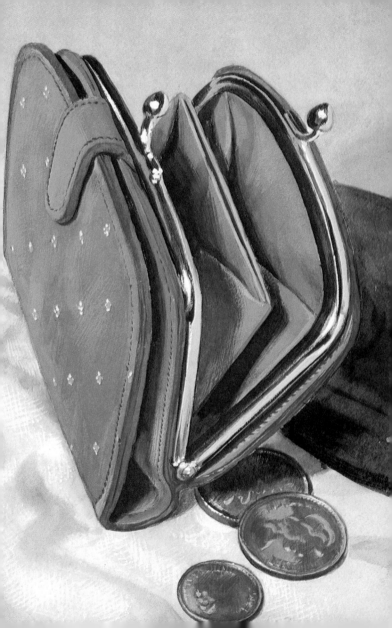

monkey

Talking about monkeys:

Monkeys are very good at climbing, aren't they?
This one is reaching through the wire.
What do you think it is reaching for?

32

basket

Talking about baskets:

What is the girl taking home in her basket?
How many oranges can you see?
When you go shopping, what do you like to put
in your basket?

bridge

Talking about the bridge:

What can you see on the bridge?
What can you see under the bridge?
What do you think this bridge is made of?
Can you build a bridge with your bricks?

peas

Talking about peas:

All peas have grown inside pods like these, even
those we buy in a packet or tin.
Look how the peas fit inside the pod.
Have you ever opened pods of peas?
How many peas here are out of their pods?

penguins

Talking about penguins:

Where can we go to see penguins?
They are good swimmers; can you guess what
they like to eat? That's right, fish!

gun and holster

Talking about guns:

This is not a real gun, is it?
Real guns are very dangerous.
Which is the trigger?
Would you like to be a cowboy?

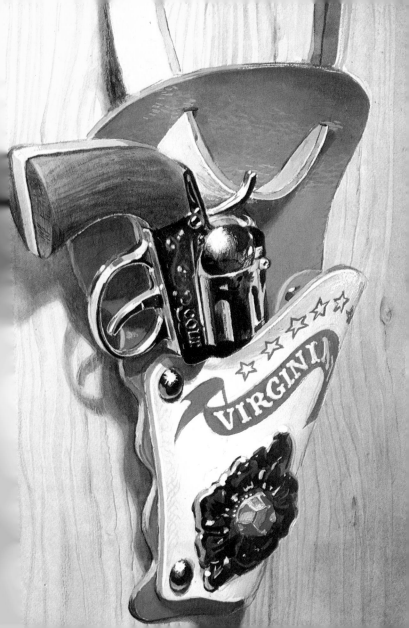

parcel

Talking about parcels:

Here is a parcel with a birthday present inside.
If it was your present, what would you like it
to be?
Do you like the wrapping paper?
You try to make a parcel.

Happy Birthday

paint
brush

Talking about paint brushes:

When we paint with a paint brush the bristles are dipped into the paint.

Do you know which are the bristles?

Which colours do *you* like to paint with?

tent

Talking about tents:

These children are playing in their tent but it is big enough to sleep in, too.
Do you know what camping is?

lion

Talking about lions:

Do you think this is a father lion or a mother lion?
What do we call the long hair around the lion's neck?
What kind of noise do lions make?
What do you think they like to eat?